Rush

Of

Many

Waters

Also by Pauly Hart

Novels:
By the Gates of the Garden of Eden
Novellas:
Superior Respondent
Ouesso to Epena
The Book of Lesser Voices
Mountain to Mountain
The Word of Yahweh unto Enoch
Empire of the Dragon
Finance:
The Richest Man In Babylon Continued Stories
Collections:
Sometimes I Write Tiny Stories
Adelphoi
Poetry:
Stupid Mind Tricks
Book of Love and Laughter
The Cross and the Poet
What is Poep?
I Love You More Than a Fox Loves Blueberries
The Night Clerk Held a Broken Pencil
Spontaneous Psalms
Kick the Prick
Exegesis with Co-Authors:
My Flat Earth
Biblical Cosmology, 8+ languages
Translations:
The Testament of Job in Modern English
Children's:
Mathmagician and Other Tales of Awesomeness
Periodicals:
Modern Epistle (1-8)
Microzine (1-5)
Rush of Many Waters (1-20)
With children authors:
Farrell Family Fables
With Co-Author Jennifer Hart:
Adulting: A Daily Guide on Being an Adultier Adult
Audiobooks:
Biblical Cosmology
Superior Respondent

Rush of Many Waters:

Volume Seventeen

By Pauly Hart

Contents

Shorts

Moth Clan

The only time he saw the moth clan was in the night. It was always in the same room, a cottage style bedroom with only a small orange molded chair and a student's desk against the wall. The walls were lime green on two sides and it was upstairs. He knew it was upstairs by how one of the walls was sloped downwards. Not all the way to the floor, mind you, but halfway, as in you would have to duck if you were to touch the wall. There was an old closet door with a white ceramic handle and a small light hanging from the ceiling. The bracket marks where shelves used to be could still be seen - where someone had hastily painted over them with the hideous green paint. Against the door away from the room stood another door, propped up against it. He had no idea how it had come to be there, only that it had. That was the way the house was.

The moth clan were snowy white. They were gentle, fragile things and they would come in through the window and fly about me, all around. They would whisper secrets to him, that he could never fully recall, and then dance and inspire him to sing and dance himself. They were the happiest moments in his life, as he could recall, and he did not want them to come to an end... But they did.

They always came in through the window. There were two dirty windows that faced outside, and both of them had an old crank that would open them up towards each other. The one on the right was always open and that is how the moth clan would enter the room and dance and whisper their secrets. The window was always open whenever he arrived and would stay open when he left. Outside the window, he could see a utility pole with a light at the top and woods all around. It was the only thing he knew about what was outside.

One night they didn't come. The light was on and other bugs wandered in and out. There was one gray moth who he tried to talk to, but it did not speak, so he left it alone and waited patiently for them to arrive. They did not come that night or the next night either. On the third night, he was tired of waiting for them. What else was there to do in the room but dance with the moths? Nothing as far as he could tell, so he opened up the closet door.

Inside the door there were six or seven dresses: old and unused and in ill repair. They looked like old women's dresses, mauve and purple and gold. There was nothing else inside and it smelled heavily of old pine. He moved to the other door - the one propped against the door to the room. It was dusty and had never been moved as far as he could tell, so when he moved it, he sneezed violently for all the dust that also inadvertently moved. It was heavy, as old doors are, but once moved away and leaned against the adjoining wall, he was able to see the door to the room finally.

It matched the other two doors. Old heavy wood with the white ceramic handle, and it was locked. The lock was above the handle in the old turn-key latch style. He flipped it, touched the knob, took a deep breath and woke up.

The red bump on Nick's face wasn't going away, as a matter of fact, it was getting bigger. He wiped the steam from the mirror with his hand, even though he knew his mom hated it when he did that. He leaned up against the sink and looked at it again. About the size of a dime and red as fire. Like a mosquito bite or something. He breathed in and slowly raised his fingers to his face. He would try and pop it again today. Or at least get the white head to show. But the instant he touched it, tears came to his eyes.

Nick wasn't a baby. Just the thought of Terry calling him one made him mad. But he couldn't even touch it. The last thing he was going to do was cry or tell his mom. He would have to be sneaky at breakfast otherwise she would put her paws all over his face and make him squirm. Maybe if he sat on the other side of the table he would hide from her.

"Get down here now!" she called again. So annoying.

He was probably late again. He ran the towel over his head and zipped out the door, down the hall and into his room before he called out: "OK, OK Jeez!"

"Don't you 'Jeez' me mister! Hurry up!" she shouted.

Ugh. Mom seemed to be regular style again today. He called it "regular style" in his mind ever since Uncle Tony had died. She was always in a hurry and always talking about money. He didn't know why Uncle Tony had changed her, but he never could figure her out. If this is what women turned into when they got older, he would never marry one, that's for sure.

He threw on something from his closet. Whoops. Not that shirt. It didn't fit anymore. OK. The red and white one. The one without the stain on the front. Alright. Pants, socks, shoes. Done. Down the hall and...

"What in the world is keeping you so long?" his mom yelled up at him.

"Nothing." Nick replied.

"Well, the bus will be here in six minutes. Here's five dollars for lunch. Eat a vegetable today." Mom said and put a plate of French toast in front of him with peanut butter.

"I will unless it's broccoli." Nick said. He grabbed the peanut butter. He hated syrup on his French toast.

"Fair enough. I didn't raise no fool." she smiled.

Nick smiled back. He thought she would yell at him for that. He cut into his French toast and put a delicious piece in his mouth. Mom made the best French toast.

"What's that honey?" She had noticed the huge zit.

"Nothing." he said, his mouth full.

"Oh? Looks to me like you're going to be growing a beard soon, huh?" she said. "Should I buy you a shaver?" she smiled.

"Mooommm." Nick groaned. That was all he needed. The only kid in school with a beard.

They both heard the bus pull up and honk. Her first action was to grab his book bag and open the door, while his was to stuff another couple of chunks in his mouth and chew like a madman.

"Go, go, go! You know she hates to wait!" she yelled from the front door. She opened the screen and waved at the driver: "He's coming!" she called.

He knew what time the bus would get there. It was always there at 7:45 with all the idiots aboard. He only wanted to sit next to Kenny and talk about Sisugi. He threw down the last of the French toast and was out the door.

Racing out the door with the book-bag and hopping onto the bus he ran like a comet. Bam. Right in his favorite seat next to Kenny.

Something, something "In a hurry!" The bus driver was saying as he got on. Whatever. Kenny had on new shoes.

Kenny sat on the third to the last row on the left side as he walked back. It was a good spot. One row back from the wheel and the cushion wasn't crap. The gross green pleather was worn in just the right way so your butt didn't complain. Kenny was already sorting cards. Sisugi was mostly a card game, but to Kenny, it was a lifestyle. All he talked about and all he drew were Sisugi warriors and monsters.

"I don't see what the big deal is." he said, holding up one of the Sisugi cards. He only attacks seven but his defense is two. He's killed before he can do anything." He plopped the card in my lap. "Shinobi Disciple" was the title on the card. He had a lot of copies of that card. It was common. Most of them he increased the cost by one and wrote a 4 over the 2. He loved to fix the cards that he thought were wrong.

"It's not bad." Nick told him. "He's fast." He gave it back to him.

"Keep it. I've got twenty of them." Kenny shuffled some more Sisugi cards. "What I'm trying to collect is the Shinobi Acrobat, Shinobi Assassin and the Shinobi Teacher."

"Shouldn't it be called "Shinobi Sensei?" Nick wondered.

Kenny looked at Nick through his glasses as if seeing him for the first time. "Yeah. That sounds way cooler."

At recess they would sort Kenny's cards into categories. Kenny didn't care that they were dirty, he just loved to sort them and resort them and find new strategies. He was never satisfied with what he had.

"Did you have the moth dream again?" he asked Nick. He had his Demons and Angels all in one pile together and Knights and Sultans in another. Nick didn't say anything at first. Kenny was the only one Nick had told but it was weird to hear him ask it like that.

"No. They didn't come." Nick said.

"That's weird." He stopped and looked up. "Did you call 'em?"

"No, I didn't think about it." Nick confessed. That was a good idea. "I opened the door though."

"Huh," was all Kenny said, and went on sorting. "I never thought of that."

3

That night the moths did not come again. He sat in the chair until he knew they weren't coming. Then he turned around and stood up and went to the door. The other door that he had moved last night hadn't been moved back, so he went to open the other door again.

It was always so quiet here. There was never any sound. Usually in the city you can always hear something. Trucks or whatever, off in the distance. There wasn't anything here. All he could hear were the sounds that he made. It was really creepy.

When the door opened, it creaked and he almost pooped myself. It was one of those funny creeks that you only hear in movies too. Like: *"Reeeeeeeeeeee!"* His heart was beating pretty fast so the next thing that he saw still freaked him out a little, but didn't actually give him chills. He was at the top of a staircase on the second floor. Hanging from the ceiling of the entire floor were fly traps. They were spaced a few feet apart, as if ready to catch an army of flies. They were longer than normal too, so he almost had to duck to miss them. They went all the way down the hall to the only other door on this floor. It was shut.

He didn't move for a long time after he saw it. You know that feeling you get when you're trying to make out something in the dark, and you can almost make yourself believe that it's a ghost or something really weird... And then it turns out to be your brother all along... That's the feeling that he got the longer he looked at the door. Something about the shape of the painting made him not look away. Something was familiar about it all... And the longer he looked, the more and more he was convinced that what it was wasn't what it was... On the door was painted a white moth.

It was then that he noticed that every flycatcher was covered in moths. This is where they had come. They hadn't come back to him because they were all dead.

4

The red bump was enormous and Nick's mom looked worried.

"Looks like we may have to amputate, kiddo." she said, not really joking, but exaggerating... It was her lame attempt at getting on Nick's level. It annoyed him but he knew why she did it.

"Thanks mom. You can keep my face in a jar by the sink so I can stare at you all the time." Nick said, a slow smile on his lips. Parents loved dorky stuff like that.

"You think I want to keep it by the sink?" she smiled. "No way, Jose'! I'm putting it in the attic and only bringing it out on Halloween."

"You wish." he laughed. "I'll break out of the attic and come haunt you."

"Hey," she said. "Seriously, we need to pop it or something. It looks grody."

"Tonight?" he asked.

"Deal." she said.

Kenny was sick and wasn't at school. It was a horrible boring day, especially Math class.

That night, Nick found a note on the kitchen table and some money to order a pizza with. She would be working late and couldn't make it home. He would have to pop this bad-boy himself.

After a quick YouTube tutorial, he got everything ready. He didn't have rubbing alcohol but figured that Hydrogen Peroxide would do the same thing, so with needle in hand, he gently pricked at the red spot.

"*AAAAAH!*" He screamed as it barely touched his skin. He looked around. Oh yeah, no one was here. He still didn't like acting like a baby so he tried not to scream the next time.

He poked in a little, the pain becoming a red fire in his mind, pulsating into his thoughts. He squinted his eyes shut and kept pushing down into it. There was a small pop and a release and hot stream of brown and green liquid splashed over his hand and into the bathroom sink. The smell almost made him vomit.

Nick pretended to be asleep when his mom got home. She came into kiss him and noticed the Band-Aid on his cheek. Turning her phone's flashlight on, she inspected it.

"You asleep hon?" she asked quietly.

He thought about answering, but by the time he had made up his mind, he was sitting in the chair in the room, in his dream.

Something had stirred him into action. Maybe it was the zit. If he could do things like this, then why not finish his dream? Figure out where the moths went? Yeah.

He was sitting in the chair. He got up and went to the hallway. There was no sound, as always, so he went downstairs. The walls were recessed wood, the kind you find in old movies, with photos on the wall. he couldn't make out any of the photos; they were all blurry, which was really weird. He walked to the front door.

It was huge, maybe as tall as a basketball goal, and the knob was almost too tall for him to reach, but he reached up anyway and turned it. It was locked. Screw that. Maybe he could go outside thru like a window or something. He didn't know what made him want to go outside, he just needed to.

Michael W. Smith's "Open the eyes of my heart Lord" went through his mind as he pulled open the dining room window and crawled up on the ledge. He didn't know why this song came to him just then… It just did.

The air was not cold, like it looked, it was the same temperature as the house. Perfect. But it was too quiet. The ultra-green grass was almost glowing as he stepped down onto it. Perfectly manicured. Perfectly mowed. It even smelled like it had been mowed today, that crisp green smell came up to my nose like a wave. Almost delicious.

To the left and right of the front of the house was green grass. There were two poles with mounted lights on them, but off in the distance, down what looked like a trail or a driveway, was some sort of red glow. He woke up.

6

Kenny wasn't at school that day either. The whole day was so boring. Nick asked the school office where he was but they just said that he had called in sick. "They didn't care." Nick thought. Kenny didn't really have any friends except Nick and it was all lies anyway. The teachers only pretended to care.

On the bus ride home, Nick sat in the front seat and asked to be dropped off at Kenny's stop. It was only a few blocks from his own house, but it would be quicker than getting off at home and walking back. The bus driver said: "No way," but Nick jumped off anyway. Silly old bus driver. Too slow for Nick.

He ran to Kenny's house and rang the doorbell. No answer. He rang again and banged on the door, still no answer. Weird. No lights were on. Nick decided to walk home when he heard his name being called. "Nick!" A voice called from the second floor.

"Hey man, you sick or something?" Nick called up. It didn't sound like Kenny, but maybe he had a sore throat or something. He could see the window open, but didn't see anyone. "Kenny!?" He called. No answer. Just the wind on the curtains. Double weird.

Mom wasn't home again so it was time for surgery. In the mirror, he checked out where he had popped the zit. He still had a Band-Aid on it, so he peeled it back to take a look… And wished he hadn't. It was gross. A yellowish black spot that looked like it was getting bigger was now in place of the red welt.

Youtube again. So, apparently, there might be a hair stuck inside there causing the infection, a couple of videos had told him. Tweezers and nerves of Superman was all it took.

He got to work on the bathroom sink. Using the same needle (sanitized with more Hydrogen Peroxide of course), and the rest of the "face kit" he went to work pulling off the old scab. More black ooze came out but he got it all, and none got on his hand this time… Whew.

Now that the scab was off, he thought he could see the little devil buried in there. If it was a hair, then it would come out and everything would be well. Or it could be a bot-fly. He freaked out a little when he watched one of those being pulled out of a guy's head. But that guy had gone to the trash dumps in India… This wasn't India, so he should be safe, right?

After what seemed like five hours, but was only twenty minutes, he gave up. He had made the hole larger and all that showed underneath was a greenish spot. No hair down there. Nothing. It was really weird. Just some grayish puss and a bright green spot.

7

He started right where he left off last night. The driveway didn't look like a driveway that he had ever seen, it was just two rough grooves in the lawn. He walked down it. The red glow was still out there and it was still night. As he grew closer, he started hearing sounds. That was super freaky because he hadn't heard any sounds at all from anywhere in this whole dream. And he'd had this dream every night for the last several months.

A low whining, like babies crying, like a whole bunch of babies crying. But it wasn't like real sound. It was like with every footstep I took closer towards the red glow, someone was turning the volume up. Sound wasn't working right, it was going up way too fast.

It was a fire, and there were people around it, doing some kind of dance or something. It looked like a weird ceremony from a lost tribe in the middle of nowhere or something. he imagined the tribe people of some ancient forest, it was so weird. They were all dancing around the fire and a huge totem pole. A Totem pole of a snake with arms.

He stopped and watched them. This was really too weird. The men all had on dog coats or something, with the dog heads still on them, like those old Roman soldiers, with wolves heads as hats. Creepy as fuck. Sorry. Not supposed to say fuck. Mom gets really angry when I cuss like she does.

They were going in a circle, really slowly, arms down to the ground, and then they spun left, then raised their arms up and spun again.

He made myself stop walking because he realized that he was still getting closer without realizing it. He told his feet: "stop moving" but they didn't. He was walking towards the fire without wanting to.

The totem pole slowly turned and looked at me. It was massive with long gangly arms and blank eyes. It reached out its hand to me...

8

Nick woke up and ran to the bathroom just in time to vomit into the toilet. Weird cereal chips like raisin bran came spilling out along with a gray sludge. He vomited again and this time it was more of the same. The stench was horrendous which made him vomit even more until there was nothing left to vomit. Snot ran down his nose and tears from his eyes as he spooled the toilet paper off by the meter, pawing away all the mess. He flushed again and again, trying to get the smell to go away, but it lingered.

Shaking, he went to the medicine cabinet to get mouthwash and purge the taste away. Salty tears made him close his eyes as he undid the bottle and took a big swig. Rinsing, he felt a little better. Placing the bottle down, he wiped his face with the hand towel. He put the bottle back and closed the door to the medicine cabinet.

It was three in the morning when his mother came running in to find Nick, screaming at the top of his lungs and peeling his face off. Underneath the smooth skin of a human child, lay that of a snake man.

Rancher dug his fingers into the soil, testing the damp level. He knew it hadn't rained in a while, he had just forgotten how long that while was. Was it eight or nine days now? Something like that. He would have to haul more water from the runoff. It wasn't really a creek, but something like a factory drain. He had heard sounds from the tunnel feeding it, and they didn't sound too evil. And the water he wasn't using for the carrots, he would boil and drink.

Well, for sure, he didn't drink the actual water; he only got the runoff from the steam. That was the best tasting anyway. Maybe had on it a little dust from the tarpaulin, but it wasn't mud, and didn't jump around like some water. Some water had teeth.

He was still stooped over the carrots when he heard the sounds of someone coming. Listening closely, he knew it was Farmer. Farmer always had the briefest stutter in his stride, from that bad leg he was always rubbing. His head now in view, Rancher stood and raised his hand and waved back and forth until Farmer did the same.

When Farmer reached him, he saw that he had a new satchel. Rancher pointed at it.

Farmer smiled and nodded. A new one alright. Maybe has valuables inside. Rancher pointed at the small shack he used for his house. Farmer nodded.

When Rancher went inside, he pointed to the bench and motioned Farmer to sit down. Farmer smiled and sat. Rancher sat opposite him, in the room's only chair. He put his hands together and slowly opened them, as one might do an old book. Farmer nodded and reached down and undid the satchel. It was old world, probably something like one owner before, or new, whatever that meant. He'd heard the word before but it really didn't mean anything. The brass buckles came undone and Rancher looked inside.

Box after box of "Wolf Performance Ammunition 9mm Luger 115 GR FMJ" He didn't know what all the words meant, but he knew what the ninems were. He motioned the open sign again and held his hand out for a box. Farmer smiled and handed him a box. Rancher opened the box very gently, the outer paper was fragile, but still in good condition. Inside was a plastic sleeve where the brass goodies lay. He took one out, placed the box on the floor, stood up and went to his bed, where his gun was. He clicked the side latch and the magazine slid out. He put the new bullet in. It fit. He needed to test it now.

He would not test it out on Farmer. He would go outside and test it. He smiled, went outside and fired it at the ground.

The gun didn't shatter and the bullet sounded like a real bullet. This must be a bullet.

He smiled at Farmer as he came back in. Looking down, Rancher saw 3 boxes of "50 Count" lying on the floor, and the bag had been rebuckled.

Rancher frowned. He did not think he wanted three boxes. He wanted more than three. He motioned to Farmer with both hands. "More, more" the gesture said. Farmer put a finger in the air and wagged it back and forth. "No more" the wagging said.

Rancher sat on the chair and looked at his gun. He did not have any more bullets. He only had carrots. He wanted more bullets, but did not have enough carrots to buy the bullets. Farmer should have carrots, but he never grew carrots, he only grew gourds and corn. Rancher did not like either gourds or corn. He liked carrots. Carrots hid away and bugs could not eat them so easily. Rancher loved carrots.

Rancher looked at Farmer with a side eye. Farmer returned his gaze and pointed at the bullets. Rancher nodded his head and went to the box in the corner and drew out three carrots.

The deal was done.

Poems

No, it's my pleasure

Take from this tree all that can be
I give it up to you in submission

Glean from its branches
Take all it gives

Use it in a way that is worthy
Really, I insist

Cut it up if you wish
Cord it out for fire

So that you may keep warm
It's no problem at all

Take from it every necessity
And even its fruit is yours

It doesn't matter

It's only my soul

It's only my love

Jenny

A beautiful life is a joy for the world
A beautiful girl: A smile on your face

With life so confused
With feelings abused

Prettiness is defined not in style
Nor in performance, nor in how you look

A truly wonderful smile
A perfectly honest shrug

This is beauty, when personified in life
Jenny, you're beautiful, you make me smile

Tears flow, life's grow
People show you hate

But remember the sunshine warming your face
Remember God, friends and good times

And THAT makes you beautiful.

Like a sunrise

My dedication comes free
But my heart must pay that price
I only want what is best for you
'Cause i know that is best for me

Like a sunrise at dawn
Like a moonbeam at night
You will know that I love you
'Cause faith comes out of me

It's love that shows up dear
When desperation leaves
It's the feeling of you here
Isn't that what you see

Like a sunbeam at noon
You leave me breathless girl
Like a moonbeam at night
It is faith inside of me

I have lost too much
I have gained so little true
But when you hold me dear I know
That it's your faith in me that's real

Like a sunbeam at dusk
Your love washes over me
Like a moonbeam at night

Your faith has made me free

Hater

The Hater and the Hated
The User and the Used
How many times and times
Must you be abused?

You push yourself to torment
She pushes you to choose
But give in or walk away
You lose, you lose, you lose.

You smother her in comfort
You smother her in touch
She doesn't want it buddy
She hates you for your love

Just walk away my friend
Don't push the solid wall

She's hurt and she will bite
You'll be punished in it all.

The manipulator she is
She punches every button
But walk away every time
She will call you in distress.
Love is blinded

Try and stop, be my guide
Win some lose some, kiss the bride
I believe you, let me go
Kissers killers, eat the snow

There's a dichotomy I feel with you
If you take my hand I'll be yours true
Lessons take me all the while
If I listen closely I just might smile

You will be my bride Frankenstein
With my pretty white dress, you'll be mine
You will be my bride Frankenstein
With my pretty white dress, love is blind

buzzz

"be gone foul demons of the air
fly away and be gone", said he.
flapping, flipping, snapping
at those pesky summer flies.

so he bought himself a flyswatter.
swat, swat, swat, swat.
now the kitchen it littered,
with dead insect carcasses.

yuck.

Jerisiah's Recollection

I saw the waves crashing, rising, churning
I saw the arms older, ruddy, lifted
I saw the sea stopping, pausing, thinking
I saw the eyes question, wonder, believe.

In the light of the ramrod golden sun, I saw
in the glory of Jehovah's chosen people
in the presence of the outcast prince deliverer
in the light of the ramrod golden sun, I know.

We ran towards the divide; smiling, laughing
we felt our hearts race; cheering, laughing
we caught up our children; cheering, smiling
we were free from harm, that is what they say.

I heard the chariots, saw the smoke, the dust
I cried out the warning, gave the call, the alarm
I warned of the impending doom, felt our loss, sorrow
In the light of the ramrod golden sun, I fear.

I saw the waves   stopping, pausing, lifted
I saw the arms older, ruddy, lowered
I saw the waves   churning, crashing, falling
I saw the eyes question, fear, and die.

In the light of the ramrod golden sun, I believe.

Instructions in pentameter

One day there was a pink flower
And she desperately wanted to be blue
She held her breath for a really long time
And the pink became blue, and in turn... purple!
But then she couldn't breathe!
So she sighed with grief,
And thought "Oh well, I guess I'm pink."
...She then looked to the sky and wished...
"Maybe God will tell me why I'm pink!
And she looked to the tree to find
A note from her friend the tulip!
And it said: "If you were blue, I couldn't be,
because God made us all the way we are.
If pink became blue, there would be no more you."
And the pink flower smiled.

Lines 2-14 (evens) written by Mandie Maclean
Lines 1-15 (odds) written by Pauly Hart

Sojourn

Travel to a town, learn to live
Travel gently, Sometimes gently
Leaning on the everlasting strength
Learning to live,
An insect crawls... you wonder
can I crawl as well?
I wish we could crawl that well
We might learn humility.
Traveling to a town.
To learn to grow.
A sojourn of apostolic faith.
A sojourn of love.
Psychopathic love.
Weird affection.
I travel to the town, I learn to live

but not from the law
but from the Lord
I wish I could call
I wish I could crawl
I wish I could wander into the arms
I wish I could wander into the strength.
I travel to a town
The town of faith.

Witness Eye

Lightning flashed across the sky
I am the voice of a thousand
Calling, the wind carries the sound
on the clefts of desire, I respond
Thunder rolled across the land
And I am the voice of a thousand

The curtain was torn from top to twain
And the dead were raised that day
Some weary women watched it all
Trembling and bewildered they fled the tomb
And thunder rolled across the land
For they are the voice of a thousand

False ones shall rise, they all shall fall
Three times Two thousand is this world old
Five times Four hundred in each two thousand
And the covenant rang out from the hills
From the sky, the shatter rent the Earth
and we are the voice of a thousand

Attribute to the attributes

Faith is faster than a light train
more loyal than a dog at night
sleeping at your feet
Destiny is smarter than an Einstein
more lovely than tender children
with sticky hands
Do you know how to speak the truth?
What is truth? a person is he.
Love is more agile than a hungry crocodile
more tender than an embarrassing moment
in a well known crowd
Hope is better than a good back rub
more happy than peanuts and hot-dogs
at a baseball game with dad
do you know how to show freedom
what is freedom? a person is he.
wonder is lighter than a goose down feather
more slap-happy than a sit-com
on evening t.v.
Death is more potent than a poisonous elixir
more gripping than a paperback
while baby sitting kids

Do you realize that all life dies?
Except the life that's in his eyes

Spontaneous Psalm #9

I've fallen in love with the maker of the universe
I don't care what the cops say
I've fallen in love with the maker of the universe
I don't care what my parents say

I've fallen in love with the maker of the universe
I don't care what my friends say
I've fallen in love with the maker of the universe

I don't care what my boss says

I've fallen in love with the maker of the universe
I don't care what anybody says
Cause I wanna be with you
Be with you Lord
Every night and every day
No matter what they say

Be with you
Be with you
Be with you

No matter what they say

I've fallen in love with the maker of the universe
I don't care what my cards play

I've fallen in love with the maker of the universe
I don't care how the cards play

No no no

I don't care what the doctors say
I don't care if it all comes down

I won't serve Mammon
But I'll serve Messiah
I won't serve money
But I'll serve my Lord and King

But I won't serve anything
Except God almighty YEAH!
I don't care what they say
Or do or preach or sing NO!

I've fallen in love with the maker of the universe
I don't care what my doubt says

I've fallen in love with the only one worthy of it
The maker of the Universe
I don't care what I say to myself
Or any day That I'm feeling down
And I can't even see the sun

I don't care what they say
I will serve him anyway

I don't care what they say
On American Idol
No no or the Bachelor
Who cares about TV
When I have Jesus

I don't care what they say
On the Simpsons
Or on Seinfeld
Or even on reruns of Alf

Oh the television!
(Man that thing can go to hell!)

I don't care what society says about me
No no
I'm gonna serve Jesus Christ myself
My soul, with body
I am poured out like living water
Yeah!

I wanna die for you if you want me to
But if I live I'll serve you all my days
Cause it's hard to be a living sacrifice
Of praise!

Living sacrifice of praise
I'm falling in love with you Lord

A living sacrifice of praise
That's what I am today
With the maker of the universe

I don't care what they say about me
Cause I ain't gonna squirm on that alter
No no

I'll be a living sacrifice
There's freedom with you
My savior true

And I'm falling in love with the maker of the universe
And I don't care what they say
I'm falling in love with the maker of the universe
I don't care what anybody says about me

Oh it's harder to be a living sacrifice
Than a dead one
Cause dead ones get to die
But not me…
I want you to hold me to the sky

Jesus take me home today
I want to hold you
Till the skies fall down from heaven

Essays

The path of truth

Here are the steps that we must have to release ourselves from the culture in which we live, as well as the steps that will help you find the path of truth.

First is the cry of separation. In the self-titled book of Jeremiah, chapter twenty three, verses nine and ten, Jeremiah is, as usual, bemoaning his souls anguish over the land of adulterers in which he lives. He said: "All my bones ache, I am as a drunkard because of the Lord… The land mourns because of their curse… Their course of life is evil and their might is not right." He saw the separation between him and the sins of his community. The differences between himself and his culture. He saw what was true and what was false in the world at that time.

See this now. Jeremiah recognizes his position within the social setting and sees himself as set apart. In the Hebrew language, "set apart" is the definition of "holy". We must have that cry. We have to recognize our surroundings as not part of ourselves… but rather like oil and water in the same vial, separate from one another. This is one of the largest lies that I find Christians living in. That they are the person that others see. We must understand that who we are and what we do are different from one another. We must find the pain of our sin and set ourselves apart from it, and say to ourselves: "Here is my sin. It is not part of me and I must divorce myself from it."

Secondly is the pain of understanding. Pain is not bad. Pain is a message sending service that the human brain uses to receive messages from the vast reaches of the human body. In our culture, we have been programmed to believe that we must stop pain at all costs. Quick, get the bandages! Get the local anesthetic! Cure the symptoms at all costs, but ignore the malady. Pain is good. Pain lets us know that something needs to be fixed. It is like the warning lights of an automobile. It is not wisdom to take a hammer and smash the lights out! Fix it, don't ignore it.

One of my favorite passages of scripture comes from the book of Jeremiah, chapter eight verse eighteen thru chapter nine, verse two. In this, we see that Jeremiah has already separated himself from his culture, he has seen the evil of it and now he must establish himself as a bastion of hope, a refuge, a voice. He says: "Oh that my head were many waters and my eyes a fountain so that I might weep day and night for the slain of the daughters of my people." This pain is eminent for those who wish to see the truth, the ultimate truth in their lives… For how can you help someone, how can you separate yourself from someone whom you are not willing to weep over first.

Thirdly is the goodness of God. Here we go again back to the good old book of Jeremiah. Let's look at chapter twenty three and verses three thru six. Jeremiah says that a king will reign in those days and all of Judah will be saved. The payoff of the crying. The realization of the pain. The pinnacle of the hope. That Christ is here and is our king to save us.

Hope, I believe is the path. To find yourself. To find your culture. And then to separate the two from one another. To begin to see yourself in that sinking, scary and often traumatic realization. Finding yourself there you must learn to cling to the one who is ultimately in control of the universe. Realizing that this is not yourself, you turn to another source. The source that is Christ alone.

Finding Him, you might say is the hardest thing to do. Perhaps you look at is as being found. This may be a more suitable situation to be in anyway. We don't have to do all the looking. All we have to do is call out to Him. All we have to do in our humanity is give the control over to God. For to do this we find ourselves at his feet. As the character Pilgrim did in John Bunyan's book Pilgrims Progress, unload your guilt and sin on the cross of conviction. To have been found by Jesus, is to be that wayward sheep forlorn and distraught… To have the chief shepherd rescue console and love you. Both are crucial to the goodness of God. We must find God and be found by him. Then we will be able to say with Jeremiah: "The voice of gladness and of joy… I will cause the captives to return to the land of the first." And in all of it, we behold the goodness of God.

From 1992 until 2005 I had been on a pathway to creation with two main thrusts. The first was my poetry. During that time period I wrote around 1,500 poems. Wow! That's a lot! You might say. Eh. When you cherish solitude and writing as much as I did at the time, you would think that it might be an underachievement. The second thrust was slowly piecing together my novel series. It was going to be epic. Massive and as broad as Dune or Lord of the Rings. It was a 24 part series that had all the makings of stardom in the science-fiction arena. Rather than write my first book, I sat about doing what's called: "World Building.' It's a trick writers use to craft the rules of the world into which they can insert their characters. Take Firefly for example. "Earth got used up," and now insert a variety of stories about space truckers and pirates. Quick and simple. Except that I had been building for over ten years. There was no middle ground for me. I was going to either build the best science fiction book series of all time, or nothing at all.

My goal was not to write my first book and then build around it, as we see J.R.R. Tolkien doing a little of in "The Hobbit." Rather, I was going to write my Silmarillion first and then world build around that. I had snippets of smaller stories that I turned into short stories but my main goal was to create the whole thing once I had the stage to do it. The place was the Hashirim Galaxy; a modified pinwheel galaxy out of phase with our own. I had races, technologies, currencies, languages, clothing styles, on down the list. I had favorite characters, maybe eleven good story lines and it was growing and growing every week. I would take my notes with me to late night diners and pour over my notes, adding new details all the time. I would go in around ten and get comfortable at Steak 'n' Shake, Denny's or Village Inn and start working. With a hot tea and a bowl of grits I could last up to two hours. My server would sometimes get interested in what I was doing but not normally... I would tell them straight up they were going to get a 100% tip so they wouldn't mind if I camped. This trick worked rather well and I would get around four to five hours accomplished with each visit. It would all fit neatly into my little file boxes somewhere in the wee hours of the morning and it would go right into my trunk.

I had created my own galaxy with my own people. I was very close to starting the main storyline in the world. I was very close to having Anakin Skywalker meet Obi Wan Kenobi. And yet, it was not to be. James Venters stole my car and sold it for crack cocaine. Now, I gotta let you know, I'm a pretty sane fellow, but this deal took the cake. When it was finally returned to me, smelly and nasty with a flat tire, my novel and all of my notes that I had in the trunk were gone.

I was destroyed. Crushed. Everything in my heart died right there. It was like he had killed my child. I remember my friend Olivia was with me at the time and I fell down in the street sobbing and wailing. She didn't know what to do, she really couldn't have known. I was devastated. Over ten years' worth of writing gone. Just like that. Gone. Once I finally came to my senses weeks later I cried to God about my plight and he led me to the book of Job, specifically, the last chapter. Job had his entire family and fortune destroyed right before his eyes. One calamity after another. My small plight was nothing in comparison, and yet, look how good God was to Job after the trials and tests that he went thru. Everything was restored twice what it had been before. If my space odyssey epics were taken at the hands of Satan, then YHVH would give them back to me. And not only restoration, but it says that Job's youngest three daughters were the most beautiful women in the world.

So God had used James to take the galaxy away from me. But yet He restored back to me double the reward in the flat earth. Amen.

His call is His will

Jesus is calling. Will you answer him? He has everything you need. He has everything you can really want. He loves you. He would do anything for you to believe in him, and he did. He put his life in the hands of the Roman hierarchy of two millennium ago. They nailed him to a cross. No mistake. He planned it. In that day a most horrific thing happened. All sin, all sickness and dying, all death and separation was nailed to him, even as He was to the cross.

Concerning death and the grave, it was the God-Son, the Joshua God-Emanuel-Christ being who snatched them out of the deceives claws. He absorbed death for your life. He wants your freedom. He wants it. He doesn't want your freedom for yourself, He wants your freedom from yourself and your freedom for Himself. He wants your life. He wants to give you eternal life in exchange for a measly hundred years or so on this earth. He will give you purity in exchange for your wretched, murky, diseased soul. He loves you. He wants both his presence and his power to rest in and on you, and inside of you.

His call is his will.